W9-CPA-993

# the Whispering Cloth

## a refugee's story

written by

# Pegi Deitz Shea

illustrated by

# Anita Riggio

stitched by

# You Yang

*Boyds Mills Press*

Text copyright © 1995 by Pegi Deitz Shea

Illustrations copyright © 1995 by Anita Riggio

*Pa´ndau* copyright © 1995 by Pegi Deitz Shea

Published by Caroline House

Boyds Mills Press, Inc.

A Highlights Company

815 Church Street

Honesdale, Pennsylvania 18431

Printed in Hong Kong


Publisher Cataloging-in-Publication Data

Shea, Pegi Deitz.

　　The whispering cloth : a refugee's story / written by Pegi Deitz Shea ;

illustrated by Anita Riggio ; stitched by You Yang.—1st ed.

[32] p. : col. ill. ; cm.

Includes glossary.

Summary : A young girl in a Thai refugee camp

finds the story within herself to create her own *pa´ndau*.

ISBN 1-56397-134-8

1. Hmong (Asian people) — Juvenile fiction.  2. Refugee camps—

Thailand—Fiction—Juvenile literature.  3. Refugee children—

Thailand—Fiction—Juvenile literature. [1. Hmong  (Asian people)—

Fiction.  2. Refugee camps—Thailand—Fiction.  3. Refugee children—

Thailand—Fiction.] I. Riggio, Anita, ill. II. Yang, You, ill. III. Title.

　　　　[E]　　　1995

Library of Congress Catalog Card Number 94-71025   CIP


First edition, 1995

Book designed by Karen Donovan Godt

The text of this book is set in 16-point Palatino.

The illustrations are watercolor and gouache.

Distributed by St. Martin's Press

10 9 8 7 6 5 4 3 2 1

*For Tom, my refuge*

—P.D.S.


*For Susan and Bob Aller*

—A.R.


*I helped make this book in honor of all
Hmong people, those deceased and those
who still have breath in them today*

—Y.Y.


## Acknowledgments

My deep gratitude and love go to Susan Clements Beam, who
escorted my husband, Tom, and me through Ban Vinai and supplied
many details for *The Whispering Cloth*. Working in the camp for several
years with America's Joint Voluntary Agency, Susan interviewed
refugees and prepared their cases for the U.S. Immigration and
Naturalization Service.

Anita Riggio and I both thank Dr. Jane Hamilton-Merritt, author
of *Tragic Mountains*, for reviewing our story and art. We would also
like to thank Mr. Khu Xay Xiong of the Connecticut Federation of
Refugee Assistance for finding local Hmong *pa´ndau* artists for us.
We are grateful to Mao and Yia Le and Xay and Mao Lee for translating
into Hmong our wishes to You Yang, the *pa´ndau* artist. And finally,
thanks to You Yang, who beautifully rendered Mai's stitches for this story.

—P.D.S.

# Glossary

**Hmong** (*mung*) people originated in the mountains of Southwest China more than four thousand years ago and have populated the hills of northern Vietnam, Laos, and Thailand. About two hundred thousand Hmong refugees now live in the United States.

**Pa'ndau** (*pah NOW*) means "flowery cloth" in Mai's Hmong language. It is an embroidered tapestry that may include traditional patterns, images of wildlife and plants, or a story. In America, quilting is a similar folk art.

**Paang Mahk** (*pang*) means "expensive," and (*mock*) means "too" or "very" in the Thai language. In Thailand, people negotiate the cost of most foods and services.

**Baht** (*bot*) is Thai money. One *baht* equals about 4 cents. The traders paid 400 *baht* — about 16 U.S. dollars — for Grandma's *pa'ndau*. Such *pa'ndau* now sell in America for at least $50.

The **Mekong River** (*MAY kong*) originates in Southwest China, courses south through Laos, and forms a long length of the border between Laos and Thailand. It continues south through Cambodia and Vietnam and empties into the South China Sea. Communist soldiers in Laos regularly ambushed Hmong refugees who tried to cross the Mekong to Thailand.

### Foreword

Refugees, like the Hmong people featured in *The Whispering Cloth*, are people without a homeland. Often facing death because they look different or have different beliefs, refugees flee their countries for a better life. Unfortunately, it may take refugees many years to find a country that will accept them.

*The Whispering Cloth* takes place in Ban Vinai, a refugee camp near Chiang Khan, Thailand. The camp has housed Hmong since 1976. Using deadly gas, poisoned nails, and ground and air strikes, the Lao Communist government has driven the Hmong out of Laos for fighting alongside American soldiers during the war in Vietnam and Laos.

Ban Vinai closes completely in 1995. Tens of thousands of refugees will be moved to other camps and eventually "repatriated" to Laos against their will. Many Hmong children may never know freedom.

After Mai's cousins moved to America, Mai passed the days with Grandma at the Widows' Store, watching the women do *pa'ndau* story cloths.

She loved listening to the widows stitch and talk, stitch and talk—mostly about their lives back in Laos, and about their grandmothers' lives in China a hundred years ago.

All Mai could remember was life inside the refugee camp, where everyone seemed to come and go but her.

"Mai!" came Grandma's crackly
voice. "Put Cousin's letter away.
The words will disappear if you read
them one more time. Come help me
with the *pa´ndau* borders."

"But I don't know how."

Grandma threaded a needle and
wrapped her hand around Mai's.
"Push the needle up through the cloth,"
Grandma instructed. "And poke it
back in when it has gone the length of
a grain of rice."

For many weeks, Mai practiced
stitching, stitches that were short and
straight, ones that looped inside others,
ones that twirled into long strands, and
stitches that looked like dots.

"Beautiful," praised Grandma,
amazed at Mai's skill. "You are ready
to go on."

Grandma then began drawing herbs and animals on the *pa´ndau* borders for Mai to embroider. By the end of the hot season, Mai was drawing and stitching her own border designs—vines of milky jasmine, bursts of purple orchid, palm trees plump with papaya.

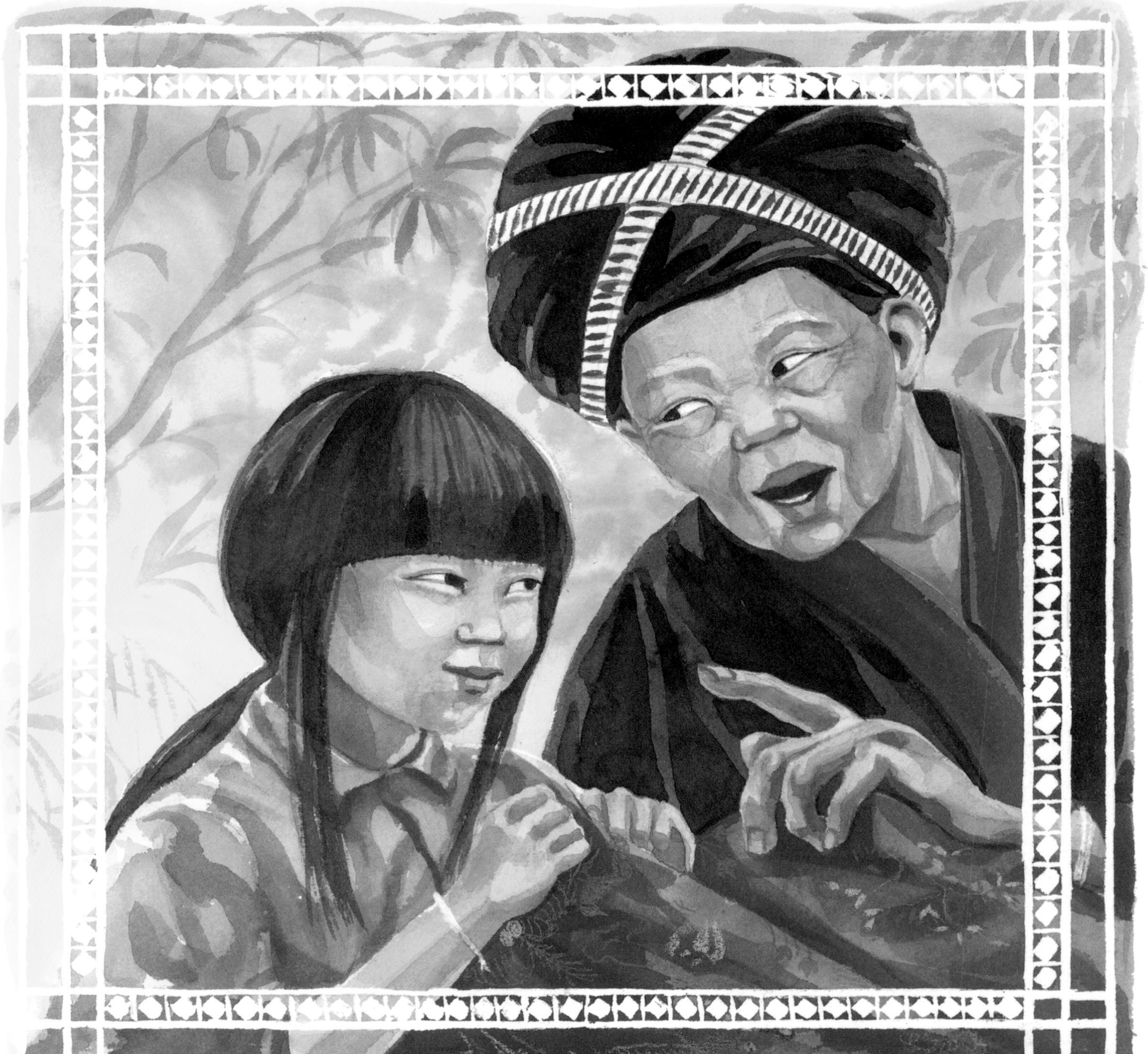

"Hurry and finish, Mai," Grandma said one day. "The traders will be coming soon from Chiang Khan."

"How much will they pay for the ones I helped on?" Mai asked, knotting her last stitch.

"Twice as much as the others," Grandma bragged. "You sew even better than your mother did when she was alive. And her *pa´ndau* were prized throughout the hills."

"*Paang paang! Paang mahk!*" the traders complained when Grandma demanded 500 Thai *baht* for her *pa´ndau*. But when they saw the fine detail of the borders, the traders agreed to pay 400 *baht* — twice the usual price.

"Keep stitching, Mai," Grandma said when the traders left. "And we'll fly from this camp before the rabbit breeds again."

Mai's hands went back to work on the borders. But her eyes and ears were drawn to the tribal stories the women stitched *inside* the borders. Every time the wind rippled the *pa´ndau* hanging at the Widows' Store, Mai heard words in the air.

"Grandma, I want to do a whole *pa´ndau* myself," she said finally. "Can you give me a story?"

"If you do not have a story of your own, you are not ready to do a *pa´ndau*."

Mai tried for days to think of a story she could stitch. But all the good ones were already whispering around her.

One night, Mai's fingers cramped so much that she couldn't sleep. Grandma lay down on the mat beside Mai, enfolded her, and rubbed her hands.

Grandma's soothing made Mai remember how she had slept when she was little, snug as a banana in a bunch. Snug…with her mother behind her, her father in front of her. Mai's lower lip began to quiver.

"I want my mommy and daddy," she cried softly.

"I know, I know…," Grandma said. "Call to them, Mai. Call their spirits with the words in your fingers."

Mai closed her eyes and tried to picture her parents. Flashes, noises, smells bombarded her. A story was erupting in her head—a story she could stitch.…

Little Mai slept between her mother and father, who were very beautiful even though blood dripped from their heads.

Grandmother put Mai in a basket on her back and ran through the paddies to the riverboats.

*Soldiers fired. Bullets whistled over the people's
heads and made rings in the brown Mekong.
On the other side of the river, soldiers in different
clothes took them to a crowded village inside a tall fence.*

People stood in long lines to get little bags of rice and dried fish.

Mai grew taller. She passed the days watching the blacksmiths make knives and tools. Sometimes she pounded balls of silver into flat sheets for the jewelry maker.

She helped Grandmother grow chilies and coriander.
Mai searched for empty glass bottles. When she
put them upside down in the ground around her hut,
they sparkled.
This is how Mai lived for many years.

Mai finished her *pa´ndau* as the rainy season was ending. "Grandma, how much will the traders pay for my *pa´ndau*? Enough to fly to America?"

Grandma ran her fingers over the needlework. Then she took the *pa´ndau* by the corners and held it up to the breeze. She turned her head so that her good ear grazed the stitches.

After a long time she whispered, "The traders will offer nothing."

"Nothing?" Mai cried in frustration.

"The *pa´ndau* tells me it has not finished its story," Grandma replied.

"But I have nothing left to tell."

Grandma squinted, pushing yellow through the eye of a needle. "There is always more thread."

Mai grabbed her *pa´ndau* and ran
through the muddy lanes of brown
huts all the way to the camp border.

There, rainwater gushed freely through
the barbed fence and joined a stream beyond.
Mai stood in the water and let it wash
over her feet. She stared out past the fence for
a long time. Then she sat down on the bank
and began to stitch.

One day, Grandmother and Mai flew inside an
airplane. They glided softly above boxes of land to a
village where homes were big as mahogany trees.

Mai and her cousins built men with white
crystals, swam in curling salt water, read books with
beautiful pictures.

*And at night, Mai snuggled with Grandmother in
a yellow bed with a silky roof.*

Many days later Mai rejoined the
women at the Widows' Store and
showed them her finished *pa'ndau.*
"It is very fine," Grandma said.
"I like the bed with the roof."
"How much will the traders give me?"
"It is worth much….What do you think?"

Mai picked up the *pa'ndau,* but
the wind blew it back against
her. The short, rough stitches
of her father's hand stood up
from the cloth to stroke Mai's
chin. She tried to speak, but
the smooth stitches of her
mother's cheeks hushed
her lips.
"Mai?" Grandma nudged
her. "How much?"

"Nothing," Mai whispered, clutching
the story cloth.
"Nothing?"
"The *pa´ndau* tells me it is not for sale."